D0758337

TRADITIONAL STORIES OF THE SOUTHWEST NATIONS

BY SAMANTHA S. BELL

CONTENT CONSULTANT
Anita Poleahla
President and Co-founder
Mesa Media

Core Library

An Imprint of Abdo Publishing
abdopublishing.com

Cover image: A Navajo storyteller wearing traditional
clothing performs on a stage.

abdopublishing.com

Published by Abdo Publishing, a division of ABDO, PO Box 398166,
Minneapolis, Minnesota 55439. Copyright © 2018 by Abdo Consulting
Group, Inc. International copyrights reserved in all countries. No part of this
book may be reproduced in any form without written permission from the
publisher. Core Library™ is a trademark and logo of Abdo Publishing.

Printed in the United States of America, North Mankato, Minnesota
042017
092017

Cover Photo: Marilyn Angel Wynn/NativeStock
Interior Photos: Marilyn Angel Wynn/NativeStock, 1; WorldFoto/Alamy, 4–5; North Wind
Picture Archive, 6; Red Line Editorial, 9; Emma Jones/Shutterstock Images, 12–13, 43; akg-
images/Werner Forman/Newscom, 14; Anton Foltin/Shutterstock Images, 17; Robert Alexander/
Archive Photos/Getty Images, 20–21, 32, 45; Deep Desert Photography/Shutterstock Images,
23; Josemaria Toscano/Shutterstock Images, 26; Jason Lewis/Dorling Kindersley/DK Images, 27;
Nancy Greifenhagen/Alamy, 28–29; Brent Stirton/Reportage Archive/Getty Images, 34–35; Corbis
Historical/Getty Images, 37; Bill Clark/Roll Call/Getty Images, 39

Editor: Arnold Ringstad
Imprint Designer: Maggie Villaume
Series Design Direction: Ryan Gale

Publisher's Cataloging-in-Publication Data

Names: Bell, Samantha S., author.
Title: Traditional stories of the Southwest nations / by Samantha S. Bell.
Description: Minneapolis, MN : Abdo Publishing, 2018. | Series: Native American
   oral histories | Includes bibliographical references and index.
Identifiers: LCCN 2017930249 | ISBN 9781532111778 (lib. bdg.) |
   ISBN 9781680789621 (ebook)
Subjects: LCSH: Indians of North America--Juvenile literature. | Indians of North
   America--Social life and customs--Juvenile literature. | Indian mythology--
   North America--Juvenile literature. | Indians of North America--Folklore--
   Juvenile literature.
Classification: DDC 979--dc23
LC record available at http://lccn.loc.gov/2017930249

CONTENTS

CHAPTER ONE

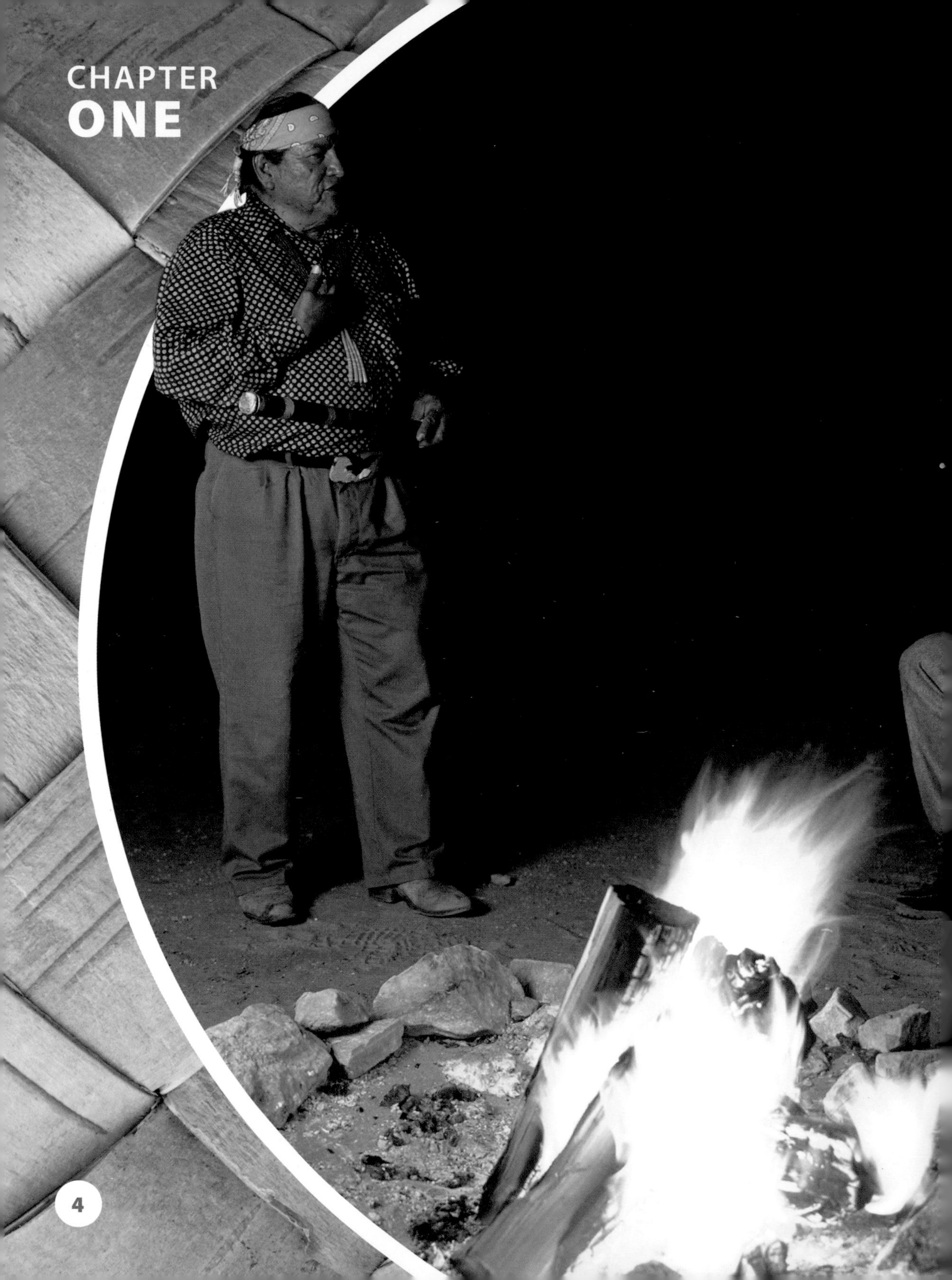

TELLING TALES

I t's another cold winter night in the American Southwest. A group of people has gathered around a skilled storyteller. Some of the stories he tells are dramatic and exciting. Others are funny. The audience settles in. They are looking forward to the adventures of Coyote and other favorite characters.

ANCIENT TRIBES OF THE SOUTHWEST

The Southwest is a land of rugged mountains, evergreen forests, and hot, dry deserts. The region has been home to Native American Nations for thousands of years.

The ancestors of today's tribes had large communities that lasted for more than

Navajo storyteller Wally Brown tells a story around a fire.

An artist's impression of Southwest Nations farmers

1,000 years. From 300 BCE to 1300 CE, they built towns and irrigation systems. They grew cotton, corn, beans, and squash. People from different communities met and traded with one another.

But around 1300, the land suffered a severe drought. With no water, the people were forced to leave their towns and move to other places. Then, around

1500, the ancestors of the Navajo (Diné) and Apache people came into the area from Canada. The lifestyles and cultures of the tribes developed in different ways depending on where they settled.

SOUTHWEST REGIONS

The two major rivers in the Southwest are the Colorado River and the Rio Grande. These rivers create four different environmental regions. The largest is the desert basin and range. It reaches across the states of Arizona and New Mexico. Most of this area is a desert covered with shrubs and cacti. Some places get less than 5 inches (13 cm) of rain a year. Tribes here, such as the O'odham and the Yuma (Quechan), have traditionally farmed, caught wild game, and eaten wild plants, including agave and the fruit of cacti.

Another region is the Colorado Plateau. It includes the area where New Mexico, Arizona, Colorado, and Utah meet. The land is made up of mountains, canyons, and forests. Lower areas have shrubs and grasses. Tribes in this area such as the Yuma, the Navajo, the Hopi, and the Zuni built permanent villages.

The Rocky Mountain region is east of the Colorado Plateau. The land has rugged mountains with thick forests of evergreen trees. Because of the cooler temperatures and short growing seasons, the tribes in this area did not spend much time farming. Instead, they hunted in the forests and found plants to eat. Many Pueblo lived in this area, as well as some Apache.

The central mountains zone makes up a fourth region. This area cuts across the middle of Arizona and western New Mexico.

A VALUABLE CROP

Agaves are plants with long, stiff leaves. The leaves often have sharp teeth along the edges. The plants range from a few inches to more than 12 feet (3.5 m) tall. They grow well in rocky soil in dry climates. The Apache and other tribes depended on the agave plants. Not only were they used for food, but tribes also used the plants to make baskets, mats, and sewing needles. Some even grew crops of agave in large fields.

NATIONS OF THE SOUTHWEST

HAVASUPAI
HOPI
JICARILLA APACHE
NAVAJO
TIWA
TEWA
TOWA
MOJAVE
ARIZONA
ZUNI
PIRO TIWA
YAVAPAI
MARICOPA
NEW MEXICO
YUMA
COCOPA
MIMBREÑO APACHE
CHIRICAHUA APACHE
MESCALERO APACHE
PIMA

N
W E
S

The Nations of the Southwest traditionally had different lifestyles depending on the region where they lived. Sometimes they traded with one another. What kinds of things do you think they might have traded?

The climate is cool, and most of the land is sloping and steep. Similar to the Rocky Mountain region, the growing season in the central mountains is short. Tribes such as the Yavapai and Western Apache used the wild plants and animals in the forests for food.

MANY CULTURES

Though the Native Americans of the Southwest lived in different climates and developed different cultures, the tribes were often in contact with one another. They traded and sometimes moved from one area to another.

TELLING STORIES

Eldrena Douma is a modern Pueblo storyteller. She grew up on the Laguna and Hopi tribal lands and often heard Pueblo stories and songs. Her favorite stories are those told by her Tewa-Hopi grandmother. Through Douma's stories, listeners can begin to understand how history and folktales are still important to Native American tribes and families today.

When resources were low, one tribe might raid another. All this contact means that many of the tribes shared common ceremonies and ideas.

Today, the nations in the Southwest maintain their unique cultures. Part of how they do this is through the stories they tell.

These stories are passed down from generation to generation. Within the stories are natural landmarks and sacred places. There are religious beliefs and ceremonies. There are lessons for living a good life. There are events that tell the history of the people. By preserving these stories, the southwestern Nations continue to preserve their customs and identities.

STRAIGHT TO THE
SOURCE

Pueblo storyteller Leslie Marmon Silko describes the role of oral stories in bringing people together:

> *The river's the one place where things can happen that can't or won't ordinarily happen in the middle of the village. . . . All of these stories and all of these things come together and the river takes on a kind of identity and becomes a very special place. . . .*
>
> *You know, a lot of people make a mistake when they hear me talk and they hear me laugh about the storytelling and I think they're confused, they don't understand. . . . But it's very important, and it's not just gossip and those aren't just stories. It's the whole basis for what keeps the people together.*

Source: "Running on the Edge of the Rainbow." *Words and Place*. University of Arizona, n.d. Web. Accessed October 31, 2016.

What's the Big Idea?
In this passage, Silko explains one role of oral stories. How does she show that she believes they are important?

CHAPTER
TWO

THE CREATION OF THE WORLD

In southwestern creation stories, the world is often made by powerful beings. These beings formed the first people. But many times the beings had to separate the men and women until they decided to get along. In the southwestern tribes such as the Navajo, men and women traditionally had different roles. But they made decisions together and treated each other with respect as equals. The following creation story is from the Navajo.

Some traditional stories discuss the creation of the unique landscapes of the Southwest.

FOUR WORLDS

In the First World, six beings lived in total darkness. They were First Man, First Woman, Salt Woman, Fire God, Coyote, and Begochiddy. One being, Begochiddy, formed mountains in the First World. He created insects and plants. But the six beings did not like the darkness.

Begochiddy told First Man to gather everything together. Then Begochiddy planted a hollow Big Reed. The Reed grew, and the beings climbed into it with everything Begochiddy created. It grew until it reached the Second World.

In the Second World, Begochiddy made more mountains, plants, and clouds. Everyone was happy for a while. Then things began to go wrong. Some people lived in the Second World, and they began to fight Begochiddy. He planted another Big Reed. They put everything into the Reed. It grew until it reached the Third World.

Supernatural figures and creation stories also appear in Navajo artwork.

In the Third World, Begochiddy made rivers, trees, birds, lightning, water animals, and more human beings. Everything spoke the same language. But the men and women argued, so Begochiddy put the men on one side of a river and the women on the other. They soon realized they were unhappy without each other, so Begochiddy brought them back together.

Water began to flood the Third World. Begochiddy again put everything he created in the Big Reed. The Reed grew, but it did

PERSPECTIVES

SPIDER WOMAN'S BLESSING

In a Hopi creation story, men and women are separated. At the beginning of time, Spider Woman controlled the underworld. Men and women were foolish and would not stop arguing. They moved to opposite sides of a river. The underworld was dark and unpleasant, and it began to flood. The people made a prayer stick and gave it to Spider Woman. She saw they had earned the right to go to a good place. She planted a reed that grew and broke through to the upper world. The Locust was the first to go through, calmly playing his flute.

In the creation story, the mountains are some of the first things to be created.

not grow high enough. The water kept rising. Finally, Locust broke through into the Fourth World with his head. Begochiddy climbed through the hole and onto an island. There were other beings with great power. They made the waters recede so there was more land.

Begochiddy put the mountains, the sun, the moon, and the stars in place. He told the people how to live and how to care for the plants. He gave them many different languages and sent them to live in different places. At this time, a being called Changing Woman came into existence. She became the people's greatest friend, and she helped protect them in the Fourth World.

ROLES OF MEN AND WOMEN

In the story of the Four Worlds, the men and women argue. After living apart for a while, they find out they need each other. In some stories, they promise to live in harmony. In the Navajo and other southwestern tribes, men and women have different roles. But the roles are balanced and respectful.

Changing Woman is one of the Holy People in the Navajo religion. In some stories, she creates the first Navajo clans. In Navajo society,

NAVAJO WEAVING

Spanish settlers came to the Southwest in the 1500s. They brought domestic sheep with them. The Pueblos used the wool for weaving, and they taught the Navajos how to weave as well. Navajo women learned to spin the wool, dye the threads, and weave them together on a loom. They made clothing, blankets, and rugs. Some of the blankets feature stripes in four colors, including white, red, dark brown, and blue. The number four is important in Navajo songs, stories, and symbols. Woven products made by Navajo people are still popular today.

a person's clan identity comes from the mother's family line. Traditionally, the women owned the land, the houses, and the livestock. Property was passed down from mother to daughter. When two people got married, the man went to live in his wife's home. Women were also the weavers and potters of the tribe.

Men had important roles too. They were the hunters and the warriors. They were in charge of farming and government. They made jewelry. They were also the ones who led religious ceremonies.

FURTHER EVIDENCE

Chapter Two describes the roles of men and women among the Navajos. What is one of the main points about their roles? What evidence is included to support this point? Read the article at the website below. Does the information on the website present any new evidence?

ROLE OF WOMEN

abdocorelibrary.com/southwest-nations

CHAPTER
THREE

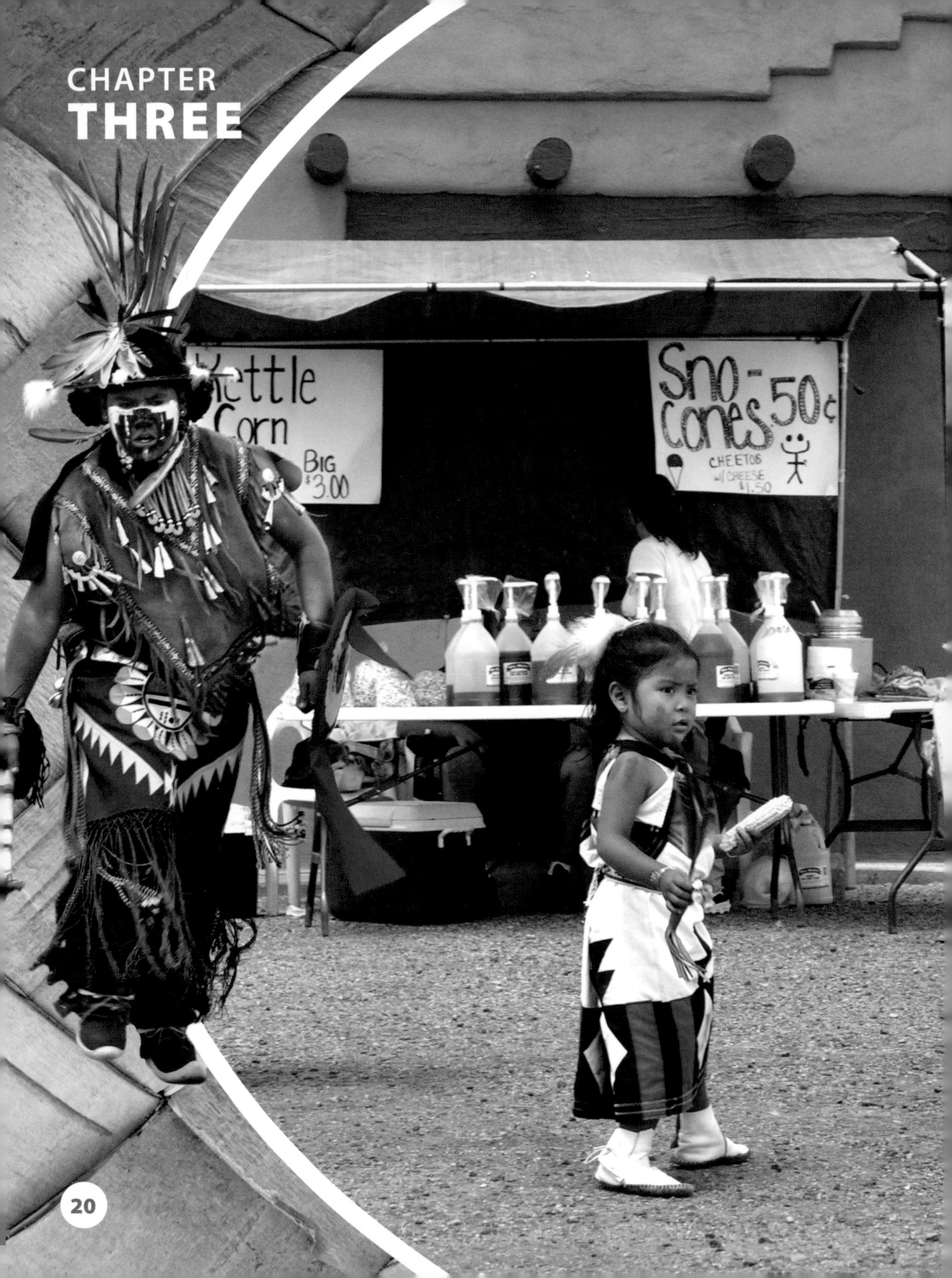

THE FIGHT AGAINST GIANTS

The word *pueblo* is Spanish for "village" or "town." It is used to describe certain Native American villages in the Southwest and the Native American tribes who live in them. The Zuni are one of the Pueblo tribes. Rainfall in their region is unpredictable. Spring and fall are the driest times. The Zuni needed rain for their crops to grow. In the following Zuni story, heroic characters rescue the rain for the people.

Zuni people perform a traditional dance at a visitor center in New Mexico.

THE HERO TWINS AND THE SWALLOWER OF CLOUDS

When the world was still new, a giant lived on the cliffs. He caught the clouds and squeezed them into his mouth to drink. The people called him Swallower of Clouds. But the clouds were necessary to bring water to Earth. The people knew the giant had to be destroyed. When the bravest men went out to kill the giant, they were never seen again.

Soon the snow stopped falling in the north. The rain stopped coming from the west. The springs in the south dried up, and the

ZUNI VILLAGE FARMING

The Zuni and other Pueblo tribes lived in permanent villages where they farmed. Corn, beans, and squash were the most important crops. The tribes developed irrigation systems to keep their crops watered. They also used farming techniques that conserved water. One method used pumice, a lightweight rock. Pumice absorbs water like a sponge. It can release the water slowly over time. The tribes used pumice as mulch to keep the moisture in the soil.

Many species of spider, including the western spotted orb weaver, are native to the Southwest.

mist above the mountains disappeared. The people's crops dried up and died.

The Hero Twins saw what was happening. They decided to kill the giant. As they walked along the path toward the cliffs, they saw Grandmother Spider. She told them the giant's trick. The giant stretched out on top of the cliffs and pretended to sleep. His legs arched over the trail. When someone passed under them, the

THE BROTHERS AND THE GIANT

In an Apache story, two brothers named Killer-of-Enemies and Child-of-the-Water went hunting and killed a deer. When they started cooking the meat, Giant came. He took the meat, but Child-of-the-Water took it back. They decided to fight. Each one would shoot four arrows. Giant shot his arrows first. They were as big as pine trees. With each shot, Child-of-the-Water faced a different direction and said, "Phoo!" Every arrow shattered as if lightning had struck it. Giant was dressed in four jackets of flint. Each time Child-of-the-Water shot an arrow, a jacket fell to the ground. His last arrow went through the fourth jacket, and Giant was killed.

giant grabbed them and threw them off the cliff.

Grandmother Spider had an idea. She went to the giant first and let herself down on his forehead. She wove a web across his eyes so he couldn't open them. Then the Hero Twins arrived. The giant told them he was too old and tired to move, so they should just pass under his legs. Instead, one twin ran to the right and one ran to the left. The giant could not open his eyes. He tried to hit the twins, but he missed. The twins hit the giant with their clubs. They killed Swallower of Clouds and threw him over the cliff.

The clouds could pass through the mountains again. Snow fell, and the rain came again. The mists formed above the mountains. The springs flowed, and the crops grew.

PUEBLO VILLAGES

In the story, Swallower of Clouds lived on the cliffs. The Zuni tribe built their homes above the floodplains. These pueblos were created on low hills, mesa tops, and ridges. The Zuni used stones and plaster to build walls. They arranged the buildings in blocks with streets between them.

The homes of the Zuni and other Pueblo tribes were like apartments. They had sleeping rooms and storage rooms. The buildings had a stepped arrangement. Some parts were made up of one level, while others had two or more. Large buildings had up

The ruins of Chaco Canyon, inhabited about 1,000 years ago, represent one of the most famous collections of Pueblo homes.

to five different levels. Ladders connected the levels. Most of the walls had no doors or windows. Instead, the people entered their homes through holes in the roofs. This helped protect the village from attacks.

PUEBLO HOMES

This diagram shows what the Pueblo homes looked like. How do you think living in a home structured like this would affect a person's daily life? What advantages or disadvantages might it have?

CHAPTER FOUR

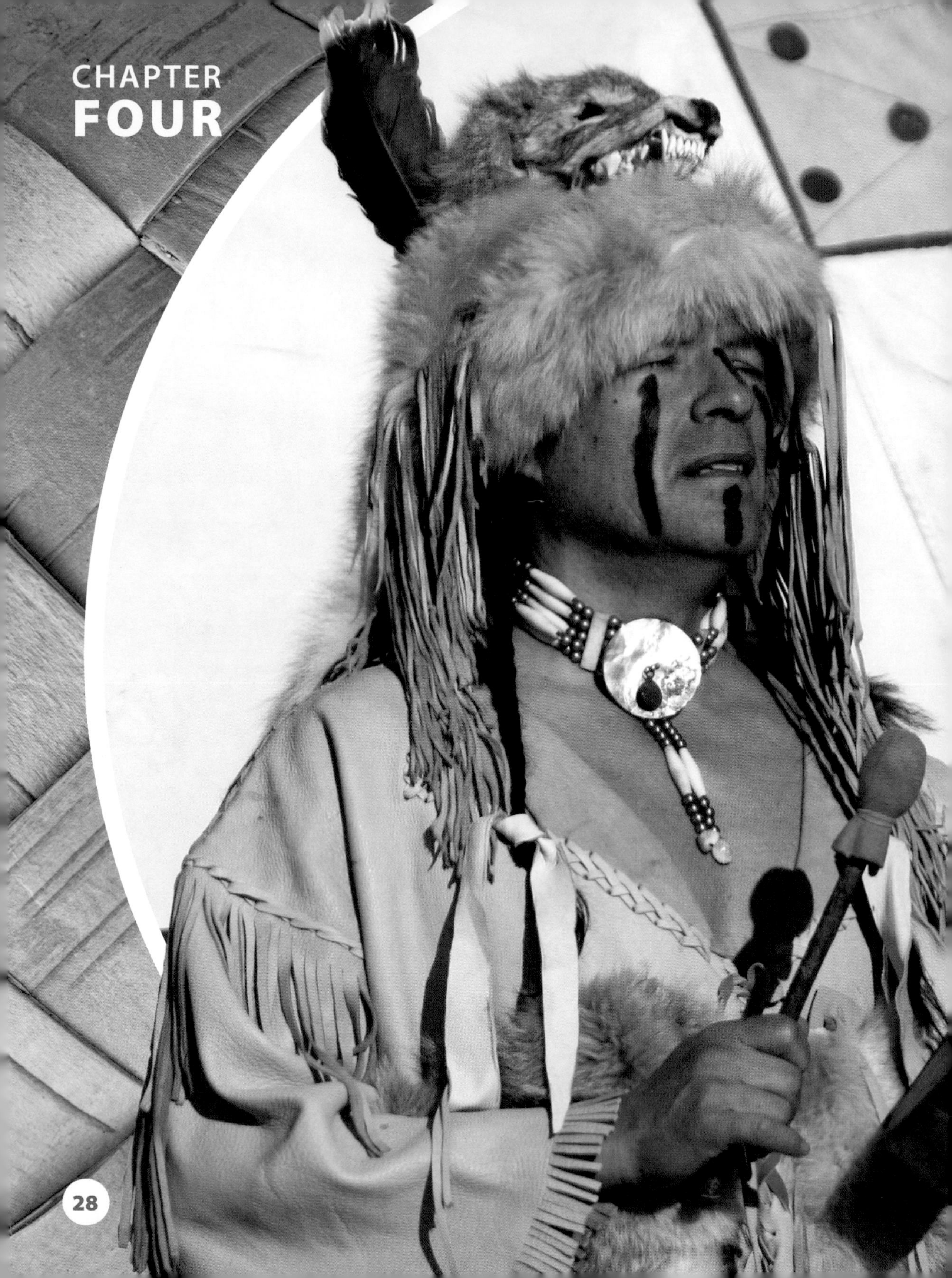

COYOTE THE TRICKSTER

The coyote plays an important role in Native American stories. The tribes respect the coyote for its ability to survive in so many different environments. Coyotes can be found in the forests, the mountains, and the deserts. Coyotes are also very cunning animals. In the stories, Coyote is always clever. Sometimes he helps people. Other times he is greedy. Most of the time, he is a trickster. He plays jokes on people or ruins their plans. In one Apache story, a group of coyotes travel together. It is no surprise when one of them tricks another one.

An Apache man wears a coyote headdress during a ceremony.

FEEDING THE TRIBE

The Apache were traditionally nomadic people. They traveled from place to place depending on the food that was available. Families often moved to find wild plants in season. The Apache hunted bison, antelope, deer, elk, and mountain sheep. They caught turkey and quail. Apaches that lived closest to the Pueblos who farmed also began to grow crops.

COYOTE'S ENEMY STEALS HIS WIFE

A group of coyotes traveled to the rising rock and set up camp. One of the coyotes had a pretty wife and a little boy. Every now and then, the coyotes went to the rock. One would get on the rock, and another would tell the rock to rise far into the sky. The rock would go up with the coyote on top of it. Then the coyote on the ground would tell the rock to come down again.

The coyote with the pretty wife came to the rock. Another coyote did not like him. He told the coyote with the pretty wife to get on the rock. The rock went up and down with the coyote on top of it. The coyote with the pretty wife liked the rock. He went up and down four times. Then his enemy told the rock to go up so high it was out of sight and to stay up there. The coyote with the pretty wife was stuck.

As soon as the coyote on the rock was gone, the other coyote took his wife and married her. He treated the little boy badly. The coyote on the rock saw bats playing above him. He begged for them to carry him back

PERSPECTIVES

MS. COYOTE AND DOE

The Navajo tell a story about Ms. Coyote. She thought she was better than anyone else. One day, she saw Doe and her two fawns walking in the forest. Ms. Coyote admired the spots on the fawns. She liked their beautiful tan coats and their big brown eyes. She wanted to make her children just as beautiful. Doe told Ms. Coyote to put her children in a small cave with a little fire at the entrance. The heat would give them a beautiful color. The ashes would fall on them and give them beautiful spots. But Ms. Coyote wanted her pups to be even more beautiful than the fawns. She found a huge cave and built a roaring fire. When it died down, the pups came out with ugly gray and black coats and beady yellow eyes.

Apache dancers participate in a spiritual ceremony.

down. One bat brought a basket with a very thin string for a rope. The bat told him it would hold him, but he must close his eyes until they reached the ground. Otherwise, the bat would fall and break his legs. The coyote agreed, and they started down. But the coyote could not wait. When they were close to the ground, he opened his eyes. They fell, and the bat hurt his shin. Then they both went on their way.

SPIRITUAL LEADERS

In the story about the coyote and his enemy, a magical rock goes up in the air and comes down again on command. Like the rock, the Apache religion had some magical qualities. Some people were spiritual leaders. A person became a spiritual leader by going on a special journey. A spirit guided the person to a certain place, such as a cave in the mountains. The spirit then took on human form. It taught the spiritual leader sacred songs and rituals. When the person returned to the tribe, he could diagnose and cure diseases.

Some tribes believed the spirit had entered the person's body. Others believed the spirit would find the person when he sang or prayed. The chants were long and complex, and each line had to be performed perfectly. Only then could the spirit help.

EXPLORE ONLINE

Chapter Four describes some aspects of life in an Apache community. The website below discusses the Mescalero Apache tribe. What information from the website is the same as the information in Chapter Four? What new information did you learn from the website?

MESCALERO APACHE TRIBE—OUR CULTURE
abdocorelibrary.com/southwest-nations

CHAPTER
FIVE

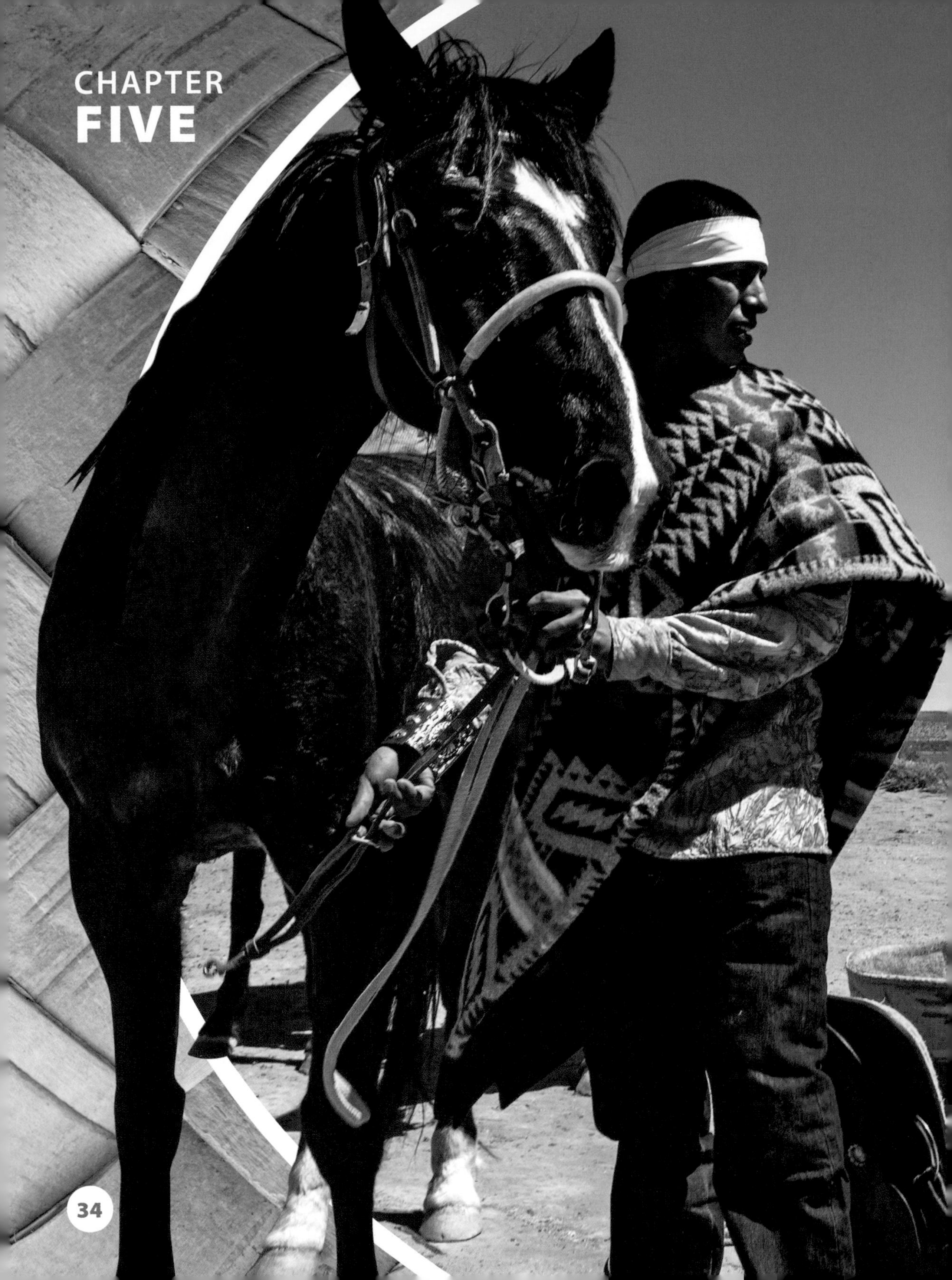

MORE THAN A STORY

The canyons, mesas, and deserts have been home to the Southwest Nations long before their history was ever written down. The oral stories of these tribes help show what they did and what they believed. For Native Americans, the stories carry special meanings.

CHANGES FOR THE SOUTHWEST NATIONS

The oral stories told by the tribes connect the people with the traditions of the past. Life for the Southwest Nations changed radically when

Stories and traditions help Native Americans connect to their past.

Spanish settlers arrived in the 1500s. The Europeans claimed the land as their own. They tried to make the Native Americans become Christians. Many of the Native Americans resisted.

When the United States took control of much of the area in 1848, the tribes suffered even more hardships. People were sent on forced marches away from their traditional homelands. Though their lifestyles were forced to change, the stories passed down from one generation to the next helped them hold on to their own cultures.

KIVAS

Kiva is the Hopi word for a special underground room in Pueblo villages. Long ago, men used kivas as sleeping quarters and meeting rooms. They are still used today for ceremonies. Kivas are all different sizes. Some are built into great houses, while others are freestanding. To enter a kiva, a person goes through an opening in the roof and climbs down a ladder to the floor.

A Zuni chief poses near a pueblo in the mid-1800s.

AN IMPORTANT ROLE

Storytellers do more than just entertain their listeners. They also teach children about behavior. Coyote is a trickster, but he can be very foolish. His actions usually create problems for himself or for others. The Coyote tales show children the benefits of following the tribe's customs. Children can also see what happens when people do not follow them.

Storytellers also provide the people with a sense of history. Before the Spanish settlers came, none of the history of the

New Mexico congressman Tom Udall, *left*, presents an award to Tewa storyteller Esther Martinez in 2006.

tribes was written down. Instead, it was preserved in the stories told by tribal elders. Religious beliefs were also passed down through the stories.

STORIES OF TODAY

Native Americans are still telling stories from long ago. They are also creating new stories. Native American authors today are writing novels, short stories, poems, plays, and films.

Similar to the oral stories, these new stories often focus on the connection between the people and the land. The land is part of who they are. The religious customs of the tribes also have a role in these new stories. The new stories are not the same as the oral stories. But they still celebrate the culture and traditions of Southwest Nations.

STRAIGHT TO THE
SOURCE

Navajo multimedia artist Pamela J. Peters wrote about why she became a storyteller:

> *In college I made the most important realization of my life: The problem with the depiction of Indians in media—the romanticized portraits and Disney-fied portrayals—is the lack of understanding of our history as actual people, Indian people. Through studying other tribal communities, I rediscovered who I was as a Navajo woman, and, with that, my purpose in life: I would become a storyteller as my grandfather foresaw. My mission: to portray the realities and complexities of native communities.*
>
> *Today my multimedia work explores the lives of real American Indians. . . . While traditions are constantly changing, I understand the strong ties I have with my culture and understand why we must maintain them as Diné people. I am grateful to be able to transform my experience into art.*
>
> Source: Pamela J. Peters. "Leaving Rez Gave Me Purpose as Navajo Storyteller." *Indian Country Media Network*. ICMN, July 30, 2016. Web. Accessed March 9, 2017.

Point of View

What is Peters's perspective on storytelling? What does she see as its purpose?

STORY
SUMMARIES

Four Worlds (Navajo)

Six beings existed, including Begochiddy. They lived in the First World, which was dark and unpleasant. Begochiddy, all the things he had made, and the people moved up into the Second World. Then they moved to the Third World. Finally, they moved into the Fourth World. There Begochiddy gave the people instructions on how to live.

The Hero Twins and Swallower of Clouds (Zuni)

The giant called Swallower of Clouds was taking away all of the people's water. The Hero Twins decided to fight him. They met Grandmother Spider along the way. As the giant pretended to sleep, she wove her web over his eyes. The Twins killed the giant and pushed him off the cliff.

Coyote's Enemy Steals His Wife (Apache)

Coyote joined a group at the rising rock. When Coyote went up on the rock, his enemy told the rock to stay high in the air. Coyote could not come down. His enemy took his wife and son. Finally, a bat helped Coyote get back down.

STOP AND
THINK

Tell the Tale

Chapter Five discusses how stories can be written down rather than spoken. What other ways of telling a story could preserve the personality of the storyteller? Are there ways to tell a story that could add something to the story? How could you use one of these methods to retell one of the stories in this book?

Say What?

Learning about the tribes of the Southwest and their stories can mean seeing words you are not familiar with. Find five words in this book that were new to you. Use a dictionary to find out what they mean. Then write the meanings in your own words, and use each word in a new sentence.

Take a Stand

Chapter Five discusses the importance of the storyteller. Sometimes stories are written and read instead. Do you think the stories should only be spoken? Why or why not?

Why Do I Care?

The children of the Southwest tribes learn from the stories passed down by their parents and grandparents. Even if you are not Native American, you can learn from the stories too. What have you learned from the stories you read in this book? How do they help you understand the cultures of these tribes?

GLOSSARY

diagnose
to recognize the symptoms
of a disease

evergreen
trees with leaves that stay
green throughout the year

flint
a dark quartz that creates a
spark if struck with a piece
of steel

floodplains
areas of low-lying ground
beside rivers that are subject
to flooding

harmony
agreement or friendship

irrigation systems
ways to supply crops
with water

livestock
farm animals such as cows,
horses, and sheep

mesa top
the flat top of an elevated
area of land with steep cliffs

mulch
a covering spread on the
ground to protect the
roots of a plant and hold
in moisture

LEARN MORE

Books

Bell, Samantha S. *Traditional Stories of the California Nations*. Minneapolis, MN: Abdo Publishing, 2018.

Cunningham, Kevin, and Peter Benoit. *The Navajo*. New York: Children's Press, 2011.

Treuer, Anton, et al. *Indian Nations of North America*. Washington, DC: National Geographic, 2010.

Websites

To learn more about Native American Oral Histories, visit **abdobooklinks.com**. These links are routinely monitored and updated to provide the most current information available.

Visit **abdocorelibrary.com** for free additional tools for teachers and students.

INDEX

About the Author

Samantha S. Bell lives in South Carolina with her family and lots of animals. She is the author or illustrator of more than 60 books for children.